EXPLORING THEATER

Advertising and Marketing in Theater

George Capaccio

Cavendish Square
New York

Published in 2018 by Cavendish Square Publishing, LLC
243 5th Avenue, Suite 136, New York, NY 10016

First Edition

Library of Congress Cataloging-in-Publication Data

Names: Capaccio, George.
Title: Advertising and marketing in theater / George Capaccio.
Description: New York : Cavendish Square Publishing, 2018. | Series: Exploring theater | Includes glossary and index. | Audience: Grades 7-12.
Identifiers: ISBN 9781502629999 (library bound) | ISBN 9781502634306 (pbk.) | ISBN 9781502630001 (ebook)
Subjects: LCSH: Theater--Marketing. | Theater--Public relations. | Theater management.
Classification: LCC PN2053.5 C36 2018 | DDC 659.2'9792--dc23

Editorial Director: David McNamara
Editor: Fletcher Doyle
Copy Editor: Nathan Heidelberger
Associate Art Director: Amy Greenan
Designer: Jessica Nevins
Production Coordinator: Karol Szymczuk
Photo Research: J8 Media

The photographs in this book are used by permission and through the courtesy of: Cover Victor J. Blue/Bloomberg/Getty Images; p. 4 Mike Powell/Stone/Getty Images; p. 10 zhudifeng/iStockphoto; p. 11, 28 George Capaccio; p. 14, 32 Rawpixel.com/Shutterstock.com; p. 17 KELENY/Shutterstock.com; p. 20 Bertrand Rindoff Petroff/French Select/Getty Images; p. 22 robbie jack/Corbis/Getty Images; p. 24 Kyle Blair/WireImage/Getty Images; p. 30 Siri Stafford/DigitalVision/Thinkstock; p. 34 SolisImages/iStock/Thinkstock; p. 41 Hocus Focus Studio/iStockphoto; p. 43 Monkey Business Images/Shutterstock.com; p. 50 Richard Drew/AP Photo; p. 54 Jewel Samad/AFP/Getty Images; p. 55 Arnold Gatilao/Flickr/CC BY-SA 2.0; p. 57 Nestor Rizhniak/Shutterstock.com; p. 60 Sparky/The Image Bank/Getty Images; p. 63 Richard G. Bingham II/Alamy Stock Photo; p. 66 Lamai Prasitsuwan/Shutterstock.com; p. 69 Granger Wootz/Blend Images/Getty Images; p. 71 pixelfit/iStockphoto; p. 74 Jetta Productions/Blend Images/Getty Iamges; p. 79 andresr/iStockphoto; p. 81 GaudiLab/Shutterstock.com; p. 82 Gregory Pace/FilmMagic/Getty Images; p. 85 SpeedKingz/Shutterstock.com.

Printed in the United States of America

CONTENTS

While a sold-out house is applauding the opening-night production, marketing and publicity people will be getting back to work.

CHAPTER ONE

Curtain Up on Marketing

It's been a terrific opening night! The director is thrilled with the performances the cast delivered. The stage manager is overjoyed with the fact that the tech crew was totally on their game, never missing a cue. Both are relieved that their work is largely over; now the cast and crew needs to do just the same thing for the rest of the run.

But not for you. In **marketing** and **publicity** for theater, while a lot of the work needs to happen before opening night, there's more to be done to get the largest possible audience for every performance. Plus, you've already started working on the next show. But right this minute, before the audience departs, you'll want to connect with the reviewer who came to cover your opening night. Better hope he switched his cell back on.

What Are You Trying to Make Happen?

Marketing—especially theater marketing—is an exciting field. The environment is fast-paced, creative, collaborative, and—no surprise here—dramatic.

People are drawn to it because they like to *make things happen*. Make what happen, exactly?

Professionals in the field of theater marketing often say that their job is to get "butts in the seats." That's their way of stressing their goal of selling out every performance. For school and college theater productions, the run is typically short, making it easier to sell out. For public theater, that's rarely achieved, unless you've got a Broadway megahit like *Hamilton*, but it's a goal nevertheless. This book will focus on the most common form of theater—community theaters—which number more than seven thousand in the United States. The applications for marketing school and college theater will be evident.

For starters, let's think for a moment about why we want to sell out. For community theater, there are a number of benefits. Filling the theater allows many people in your community an opportunity to see real live shows. It encourages actors to audition for your company again, and it rewards the tech crew for their hard work. Plus, it pays the bills.

Marketing theater requires more than just marketing the individual shows, but it's a good place to start. Here are the key marketing tasks that you'll be doing for each production:

- Identify the most important audiences, and decide what to communicate to them and the best media to use.
- Create **promotional** materials, including a poster that people will want to share.
- Coordinate and oversee photo sessions for **social media** and the **playbill** (program).

- Connect with advocates who can spread the word about your show.
- Use social media to reach more people faster.
- Write **press releases**, articles, calendar listings, and the playbill.

But Wait, There's More

While a central goal in marketing theater is selling tickets, you have a much bigger goal than just sales. You can think of it as being the **brand** ambassador. Your theater's brand is the essence of its unique story: the set of expectations, experiences, and relationships that lead someone to decide to come to your theater.

These responsibilities span the entire season, not just a single show. Depending on how your organization divides responsibilities, you may be asked to do one or more of the following jobs:

- Research the attitudes of the public as these relate to your theater and its shows.
- Select shows in partnership with the artistic director and others.
- Write, edit, and produce newsletters, brochures, direct marketing pieces, and other printed material.
- Create a publicity/press relations plan to generate greater awareness for the theater.
- Cultivate and maintain media contacts in order to generate relevant stories, interviews, and other media coverage for the company.

- Solicit, arrange, and organize media interviews (print, radio, and TV) for general stories about the company.
- Coordinate handling of reviewers, including contacting them, securing complementary tickets, and compiling press packets.
- Serve as a spokesperson for the theater.
- Organize and/or publicize promotional events and conferences.
- Maintain and update the company's website, or work closely with someone who does this.

Since it's always challenging to get a position in the arts, you can get started by interning or volunteering at a theater company to see if this working environment is right for you. People in theater tend to be very committed, so be prepared to give it your best shot. Working hard will help you get your name known in the organization and in the theater community where you live. You might also start by getting as much experience as possible in any aspect of marketing: social media, blogging, advertising, or publicity. If you can't get hired, see if you can be allowed to "shadow" a professional.

What and How

Marketing is both a what and a how. It is a series of activities, such as publicity and advertising, that lead people to buy something. It is also an approach that focuses on providing what it is that customers want.

Marketing any product or service begins with the same three essential steps:

- Provide a product/service that will satisfy customers.
- Price that product at an acceptable level.
- Promote it so potential customers will be aware of its existence.

When applied to theater, this means to produce shows your audiences will appreciate, offer them at prices that customers will see as a good value, and promote shows so that people learn about each one. This last step, promote your shows, includes a lot: social media, press coverage, posters, email, special events, and more. In chapter 3, we'll take a look at how promoting shows happens successfully.

Marketing Theater Presents a Challenge

One huge difference between marketing theater and marketing a product such as soda is "product lifetime." A can of soda lasts more than a year. In contrast, the lifetime of your "product" is limited to the length of the run. So there are no second chances if your efforts are weak. Your goal is to sell all the seats for every performance. Empty seats can't sit on the shelf like an unsold can of soda. Friday night's seats are either sold or not by 8:05 Friday night.

In 2015, *AdWeek* published an article titled "In the Data Era, Theater Marketers Can No Longer Act Like Digital Understudies." The opening paragraph was even more direct: "Marketing for plays and musicals probably hasn't been this tough since the Great Depression—even on Broadway."

Filling all the seats in your theater can be a daunting task.

The National Endowment for the Arts has done surveys to measure attendance at arts events. In 2002, 12 percent of the adult US population had attended a play within the past year. A decade later, in 2012, it had shrunk to 8 percent. The numbers are about 5 percent higher for musicals, but the challenge is clear.

And that's not all. Talk to anyone who is marketing theater today and you'll hear a common lament: the audience is getting older. If you look around any audience, you will likely see a good many gray-haired baby boomers. Thirty-somethings will be scarce, and twenty-somethings will be even scarcer.

But it needn't be that way. There are exciting theaters, like Company One in Boston, that attract young and diverse audiences. It's not an accident. It's the result of effective marketing anchored in the company's mission and vision. Chapter 3 will explore some of the specifics about how this company and other theater groups are using marketing to drive ticket sales and grow their theaters.

As you can tell by now, marketing includes a lot. Next, we'll look at three big ideas that will have you thinking like a marketing pro.

Big Idea: The Marketing Funnel

A basic marketing concept that you'll be using is the notion of the **marketing funnel**. Shown in the diagram below, it is a helpful way of thinking about the process that you'll be taking people through.

The Marketing Funnel

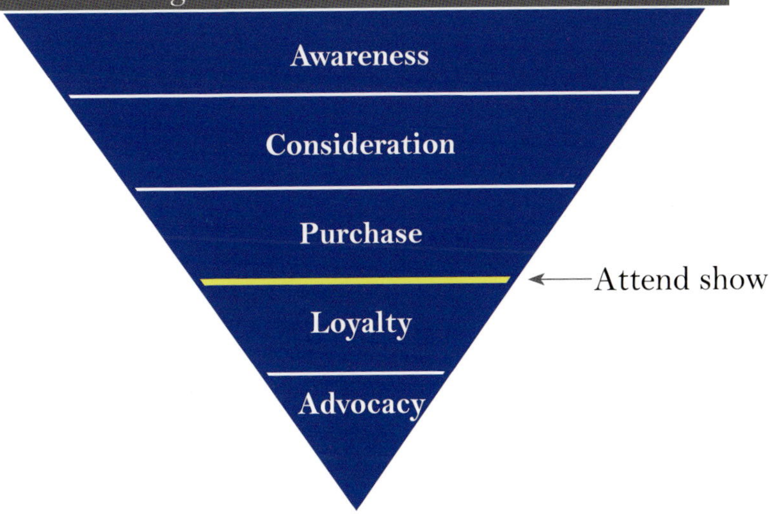

You start out with a whole lot of people in whom you want to create an awareness of your coming show. This does not mean everyone within driving distance. You want to create awareness among a **target market**: people whom you think are likely to be interested in seeing one of your shows.

Notice that this is just the first step. It's not when people buy a ticket. Very few people—and we're talking *very few*—buy their tickets when they first become aware. This is how it works: People may see a poster, and then a few days later get an email, and then in a few more days they see something you've posted on Facebook. They're now at the consideration stage. Each "encounter" with your marketing efforts moves them closer to making their purchase.

After their purchase comes their experience of your show. If they have a great time, and especially if you continue to market to them effectively, you can move them to two more stages:

Loyalty—where they continue to come to your shows and become season subscribers.

Advocacy—where they encourage others to come to your shows.

The marketing funnel makes it clear why marketing is an ongoing activity. What people in marketing think about—or should be thinking about—is not just selling tickets. We want advocates—*fans*—who will come to our shows, post pictures on Instagram during intermission, and talk about the show on social media when the final curtain falls. Their enthusiasm will not only help draw the crowds but also attract actors to audition for future shows, people to join the tech crew, and, yes, volunteers who, like you, are interested in marketing the theater.

Big Idea: The Target Market

A target market is that group of people who have the potential to buy something. Picture the people who buy and wear Nikes. It's not everyone, right?

Nike doesn't advertise on the evening news because it knows that its target market won't be watching. Instead, Nike has more than seventy-one million followers on Instagram. Nike doesn't declare that its shoes are "really comfortable and a good value," hoping that message will attract customers. Why? Because the company knows that comfort and value aren't selling points for its target market. Identifying your target helps you know whom to talk to, how they want to hear from you, and what to say to them. This brings us to the **pitch**.

Big Idea: The Pitch

Buying a theater ticket is much like buying anything else. People buy stuff because it provides benefits. It meets their needs. It's not just because it's there. You can't just tell people the name of your next play and expect them to be interested. You've got to come up with a "hook" that will capture their attention and hopefully interest them in buying a ticket.

So when you think about pitching your show, you need to think about what will get people excited. Here's an example of an effective pitch from the Cleveland Playhouse, cited as one of the best regional theaters in the United States: "*Freaky Friday*—When an overworked mother and her teenage daughter magically swap bodies, they have just one day to put things right again before mom's big wedding." That line is loaded with reasons to want to see the show. Chapter 3 will get into the process of crafting a creative pitch.

Before that, chapter 2 will explore how you can work with others to get help from some and gain approvals from others.

Great teamwork is achieved through active listening, mutual respect, and building on the ideas of others.

CHAPTER TWO

Part of a Team

Everybody works very hard, so really throw yourself into it. It'll be recognized. Theater's like a big family, and that's why I like working here: we all help each other out and do the best we can." This marketing manager was speaking for all those involved in marketing theater.

Wanted: Super Collaborators

Are you known as someone who gets along well with others? That's a good start because marketing theater requires excellent interpersonal skills. Situation Interactive is a digital-first marketing agency that promotes huge shows like the musicals *Wicked* and *School of Rock*. This company, cited as one of the best places to work, is looking for people who:

- "Are super collaborative, and enjoy being part of a team, working together to make something awesome happen"
- "Are the ultimate team player"
- "Can treat everyone with respect"

The importance of your ability to be a good team player is really clear when thinking about the fact that you will be part of three teams: theater staff, show production, and marketing.

At the start of the year, you will be spending time working with people who are part of the year-round theater staff, which will include the general manager, artistic director, **development** director (who raises contributions), and financial manager. The marketing director is involved in selecting the shows to be produced, setting goals for the year, and getting approval of the marketing plan.

A second team consists of those involved in each show, either during preproduction or production. These positions usually include the director, scenic designer, costume designer, and lighting/audio designer. There may also be a producer, choreographer, or **dramaturge**. You'll be brainstorming with this team to understand who will be the target market for the show and what story you will pitch. You'll also want to connect with the director on materials such as the poster and press releases, to be sure that you've captured his or her vision.

Who's on the Marketing Team?

The third team you will be part of is the marketing team. It may be tempting to do everything yourself. After all, who could care as much about each detail as you? The fact is, however, that you can't market a show all by yourself. Nobody can. There's simply too much to be done. It'll be a team effort.

Capturing rehearsals can provide engaging images to share on social media to start the buzz.

If you're heading up the marketing effort, before the season even begins you'll want to keep your eye out for people you can recruit to help you. Who will you want on your team? (This list of responsibilities also suggests entry-level positions you may want to pursue as you develop your marketing chops.)

Social media manager. (Also called community developer/outreach.) This has become the most important role on any theater marketing team. This person is responsible for sharing photos and videos on Facebook, Instagram, Twitter, and YouTube; responding to comments and questions that people leave online; asking questions to create a dialogue; networking with other theaters and shows online; running contests; and all the things that need to happen every day on social media.

Public relations (PR). A **public relations** person (ideally) has formed relationships with people in the media. They alert the media to coming shows and keep updating them.

Photographer/videographer. This person is needed for both publicity photos and photos/

videos for social media. If no one in your group has the right skills and equipment, you might find a volunteer.

Graphic designer. A graphic designer may be creating posters for your show, digital promotional material, email announcements, and more. If your budget is tight, try to find a talented designer who will work for nonfinancial compensation, such as tickets or advertising space in the playbill.

Web developer. Some of your most effective promotional efforts are going to be online. You will need a talented person who can keep your website up to date and who can make your most important messages easy to access. Times and dates for shows and ways to buy tickets should be the easiest items to find. As with the graphic designer, try to find someone who will work for nonfinancial compensation.

Computer guru. This person can provide computer support. He or she might also be adept at using spreadsheets, which can help you keep track of expenses and tasks. This is the person you want to have around when you're blinking at your blank screen and wondering, "What just happened?"

Working with Volunteers

Volunteers are an important part of any theater organization. The marketing/publicity volunteers will include those putting up posters, supporting social media, assisting in special events, and perhaps providing general office help. For most marketing tasks, it helps if the volunteers are familiar with your website, your brand, and your mission. (More about those later.) When working on a specific production, volunteers may benefit from having a synopsis of the script, which you will have written.

Often, people will not have experience with the specific task you'd like them to handle. It's really important that volunteers not feel overwhelmed by your request. It's helpful to break down tasks into smaller ones, give people examples of what has been done before, and encourage them to ask questions. Encourage them to be ready to teach the next person who volunteers for that job. Remember to reward your volunteers with expressions of gratitude that will include free tickets or advertising in the show's program.

What Can You Expect from Your Actors?

Famous movie stars appear on talk shows the week before their movie hits the theaters. Why? It helps sell tickets. You don't need your actors on TV—unless you're marketing a huge Broadway production—but you can ask them to use their contacts to create awareness and interest for your show. After all, actors love to perform to a full house with standing room only (SRO) for every show.

At the same time, don't expect or demand too much from the cast of a community theater; promoting the show is not what they signed up for.

You can expect help from the cast, provided you give them good stuff to talk about.

If you're marketing a high school or college production, you can expect the cast to push information about the show on their personal social media channels. In any event, just broadcasting the show times over and over again doesn't really do it. Linking to awesome photos, videos, and web content is fun, and most of your cast will enjoy sharing the promotional material if it's cool.

A bio and photo from each actor for the playbill are standard for any production, but why stop there? You can ask the actors some fun questions and use their responses for social media. They'll appreciate that you're trying to help them look as interesting as possible.

Encourage your cast to take post-worthy selfies during breaks in rehearsals and after shows.

Social Smarts Required

There's a great quote attributed to the author Maya Angelou that's packed with wisdom. "I've learned that people will forget what you said, people will forget what you did, but people will never forget how you made them feel." In the excitement of trying to make a terrific impact quickly, it's easy to accidently bruise some egos. But there are steps you can take to avoid that.

Whether you're working on a school/college production or working with a community theater, there will be others who will be older and more experienced than you. In fact, you might be the youngest person on the team that has a role in marketing the shows.

On the one hand, that's a real plus for the theater because you're part of the younger target market that the shows need to attract. You have a better understanding of what media your peers use, what offers they are likely to respond to, and what shows will interest them. You can expect that the people you'll be working with will have years of experience and their own ideas about marketing and publicity for theater.

On the other hand, that presents some challenges to you in terms of getting your ideas accepted. In joining a community theater, when you first come on board, you'll be making an assessment of what's already in place: the website, the social media **platforms** in use, the recent publicity, and so on. Your internal reaction may be, "Are you kidding me?"

It's smart to keep your critical responses to yourself until you can find a way to talk about them respectfully. The president of the board, for example, may be very fond of the website; perhaps her son designed it years ago, making it a source of pride. To be courteous and respectful, you'll want to say something like this: "Our website is so important to the marketing of our theater that it deserves to be refreshed to keep it effective. While we're at it, I have

Death of a Salesman is an enduring classic, but it's hard to make it compelling to a young audience.

some ideas for making it even better at growing our theater."

You've implied that the website is already effective—which gives a respectful nod to its creators—while softly breaking the news that you want to modify it. In point of fact, you may want to delete the whole site, but you're not going to say that. You're just going to talk about updates to make it even better. In this way, others will be more accepting as you oversee the evolution of the website.

You'll also want to be thinking about etiquette when you're in planning meetings discussing what productions to offer for the upcoming season. When someone suggests *The Glass Menagerie* or *Death of a Salesman*, you may think, "You must be joking!" or want to dive under the table. How are you going to get the under-thirty-five set excited about those plays written in the 1940s? During intermission, are they going to tweet about what a great time they are having? Possibly, but not likely.

An effective response would be something like this: "While those are classic plays that have been produced a lot over the years [a polite way of emphasizing their age], I'd like to see us do something like *Rent* that appeals to a younger audience. Let's keep offering ideas." In this way you are seen as someone who is knowledgeable, positive, and offering solutions.

Teamwork Meets Mission Statement

If your theater company does not have a **mission statement**, it's really important that one is created. A mission statement is a concise answer to two questions: "What do we do? What makes us different?" It's not enough to say: Our mission is "to provide high-quality theater."

Company One, in Boston, is a theater company that has made a name for itself by attracting an audience that is a mix of young and old and is racially diverse. How have they been so successful? It starts with their mission:

> *The mission of Company One Theatre is to change the face of Boston theatre by uniting the city's diverse communities through innovative, socially provocative performance and developing civically engaged artists.*

You can see how having this statement tells everyone what this theater—this brand—is all about. Now the task of choosing which plays to produce is easier. And the goal of marketing the theater and its productions is clear.

With this as background, we're ready to dive into all that theater marketing involves.

Avenue Q is a strong draw for young patrons at regional theaters.

CHAPTER THREE

Making Things Happen

Marketing theater is challenging—and fun—because you need to both think ahead and respond in the moment. It's also challenging because there is a lot to be done and a number of people to coordinate. In a school or college production, you may be marketing a single production. In community theater, you will be promoting:

- The season of productions and subscriptions for the season
- Each production
- Auditions for each production
- Related activities such as workshops, street theater, and drama festivals

If working with a community theater, perhaps the first place where you will be asked to insert your marketing smarts is in the selection of shows for the coming season. For example, when Boston's Lyric Stage produced *Avenue Q*, it attracted a "virtual stampede" of young patrons, shattering Lyric's box-office records that go back four decades. If you and your theater company want to attract a younger audience, you'll need to be sure your season will include shows that will appeal to them.

Thinking ahead requires creating a **marketing calendar** for the year, and then creating "production marketing calendars" with more specific information for each show.

Marketing Calendar for a Show

For each production, you'll want a calendar that starts eight to twelve weeks before opening night and runs at least two weeks after the show closes. Depending on how your company likes to work, you may want to display this calendar on a backstage wall. Of course, a digital version will be accessible to everyone 24/7 no matter where they are. Remember, you'll be relying on the help of volunteers to get things done, so you want to have a way of keeping everyone on the same page. This can be as simple as an Excel spreadsheet, or you may prefer an app. (Search the internet for something like "free task management software for teams.")

Your marketing calendar will include what information you're sending out, when, and where. Maybe you publish a blog post on your website every Tuesday, and you upload photos to Facebook each Wednesday. Your first press release may go out two weeks before opening night, and a reminder to the reviewer goes out three days ahead. Not having a marketing calendar is said to be the number-one mistake that new marketers make. By using the calendar to keep track of what needs to be done, you'll stay on schedule and avoid missing deadlines.

Here is a list of essential tasks you'll want to include on your marketing calendar for a show:

- Request cast and crew bios and headshots for the playbill (program) and for publicity.
- Contact the local media.
- Arrange for interviews with the director, principal actors, and other key people.
- Arrange for photos/videos of rehearsals for social media, especially dress rehearsals.
- Arrange for photos of the costumes and sets for social media.
- Create posters and flyers; have them duplicated and distributed.
- Create social media basics, e.g., Facebook page, YouTube channel, and a new hashtag.
- Create a mailing and e-blasts to your subscribers and your larger **database**.
- Create a playbill and have it checked by cast and crew.
- Write special articles for targeted newspapers.
- Create ticket giveaways.
- Send publicity to local newspapers and radio stations timed to appear in the final week of the production's run, reminding the public that this is their last chance to see the play. These can be fifteen- or thirty-second public service announcements (PSAs).
- Generate special announcements when tickets for each performance are almost sold out.

If you're creating a spreadsheet, here's a sample that includes who is doing what and when:

Date	Media	Content	Responsible
3/15	Facebook	Photos of set under construction	Yvonne
3/16	Blog	Interview with director	Adrian
3/18	YouTube	Video of rehearsal fun	Dylan

This calendar does not include a couple of things you need to do yourself and not delegate. You'll definitely need to read the script. In fact, you will probably want to do this while the previous play is still in rehearsal, as you may need to send out advance publicity. Write a synopsis so you can brief the others who will be working with you to publicize the show.

Another thing you'll want to do is talk to the director of the production to discover his or her vision for the show. The director's creative vision needs to make sense to your existing audiences, so there may need to be collaboration between marketing and the director. Marketing cannot be expected to "persuade" people to see something they are not likely to be interested in.

You'll want to talk to the creative team about their vision for the show, including the look or mood, and where it will be set—a charming village in Romania or the dark forest surrounding the village—so that everything you create around that production will match as closely as possible. Based on your conversations, you will be able to create a number of "stories" that you can tell about the show. These stories are often called the **USPs**, or unique selling propositions.

Creating a Marketing Strategy

Now that you've done your prep work and know what the production is all about, you should have a good idea about who is going to be interested in this show and why. At this point, some experienced marketers have a tip you can use to help you remember your target audience: Find a picture of someone who fits the profile of the ideal target audience member. Cut the picture out of a magazine or print it out from an online source, and stick it next to your computer or in your workspace.

Now get specific about this fictional customer, called a **marketing persona**. Using your best guesswork, or some research, invent a profile with important details like these:

- What is his or her age?
- What is his or her gender?
- What does he or she do as a job?
- What does he or she do during leisure time?
- Is he or she culturally savvy? Does he or she go to art exhibitions?
- Does he or she go to the theater a lot? What types of shows does he or she like?
- What websites and social media does he or she use? What newspapers does he or she read, if any?

Now that you are picturing your target—literally—you can think about how he or she would want to hear from you. Does your target audience

Your marketing persona comes alive with a photo of your target audience.

go for more traditional media? If so, you'll need to plan advertising and articles in newspapers, plus something like postcards. Or is your audience going to be reachable using social media and online content? In fact, any time you're doing anything with your marketing campaign, look at the picture and ask yourself, "How is what I'm doing targeting this person?"

Your Opening Act

You can think of your theater's website as your "opening act." When people hear about your theater, what's the first thing they are going to do? That's right: search for you on the internet. When they get to your website, they will begin to have an experience with your theater. You want them to feel as excited as they do when they watch the curtain going up.

One thing you'll want to do, if you're new to the organization, is to take a critical look at the theater's website. You may see at a glance that it could do with an update. What will make your website as effective as possible?

To improve its effectiveness, the first thing you'll want to check is that your theater's website looks unique. What is your theater's mission and brand? If you like, think about your theater as having a personality. Is it fun, youthful, energetic? Is it traditional, classic? Your website needs to convey who you are so it can feel welcoming to your target market. You'll want to start this process by checking out your competitors' websites, since you want your website to be different than theirs.

You've probably guessed the next thing that will make your website compelling: arresting, intriguing photos. After all, you're in the business of presenting live drama, complete with interesting costumes, colorful sets, and emotional lighting. Be sure to post photos that capture the excitement and color of your theater's productions. Of course, you'll want to avoid making it so busy that it looks confusing.

Next, make social **media icons** prominent on your website. This will make it easy for folks to connect to the platforms you're using, like Facebook, Instagram, Twitter, and YouTube. In fact, you'll want to include a small, unobtrusive overlay asking people to "like" you on social media or to "share" your posts on their own pages. Why? People are more likely to take an action if you come right out and ask them. Just think of how much more money that hamburger place (you know the one I mean) makes because they're always asking, "Would you like fries with that?" You just have to ask.

Be sure you let people know *why* they should see your next play. It's not enough to announce that your

Ticket booking should be three things: easy, fast, and reliable.

next play is *A Streetcar Named Desire*. You need to motivate people to come to *your* production of this famous play. As soon as you've gotten a good review, captured good quotes from your audience, been chosen for a festival, or won an award, splash that on your website, in addition to using it on social media.

It's more than likely that your website visitor has seen or heard about your show and now is checking out ticket pricing and availability. Make it as easy as possible to buy a ticket. They should spot "buy tickets" at a glance, and the process should be streamlined and stress-free. There are many options available to handle online ticketing, so be sure the service you are using serves you well.

And we can't forget the rest of your season. Be sure your visitors can easily find the entire lineup of this season's shows. Also, a showcase of your past successes, while not on your home page, will help sell your visitors on the appeal of your theater.

You'll want to be sure that your website has a page for members of the media, which will include:

- Titles and contact information for people responsible, such as the publicity director
- Links to press releases about coming shows and special events, such as a special presentation of indie films by local filmmakers or a festival of short plays
- Links to articles about your theater's various directors (costume, music, etc.)

It's really important to be sure there is a Volunteer page and that your marketing needs are included—not just costumes and set construction. As you saw in chapter 2, you'll be on the lookout for people with these abilities:

- Photographer/videographer
- Graphic artist
- Writer
- Social media

You might also enjoy doing short, fun podcasts to post on your website. These can be conversations among the cast, or interviews with directors or other creatives. Then—you know what's coming next—promote them on social media.

A Bit About Blogs

Blogging creates content that lives on your website. It has a longer shelf life than social media posts, although you can tweet links to the blog on a regular basis to keep traffic moving to your website. If you write a short article and only post it to social media, it will get buried as you post more. It is unprofessional to suggest someone go to your Facebook page and scroll through a river of posts to find a specific article. A blog makes it simple to find past posts, so you can easily refer people to them and link to them from other parts of your website or from social media. Your blog can help take people from awareness to advocacy, as we talked about in chapter 1.

Think about whether you have the time to commit to a blog before starting it, however, as it will be a waste of time if you don't post at least twice a week over an extended period of time. Whether or not you create your own blog, you could write guest posts on other blogs that your target market reads. This is a great way of getting yourself in front of potential future customers and making them aware of your existence.

Be on the lookout for someone who would love to write regular blog posts about your theater.

There is a hidden bonus with these posts. Not only will you potentially get direct traffic when prospects read your post and click through to your website, but you will also get an SEO (search engine optimization) boost from the link to your website at the bottom of your post.

Finally, invite local bloggers (with the right following) to a rehearsal during the last week before the show to watch how things are coming together and even take a few pictures. Blog posts that they write about your show help bring their followers to your website or box office.

Outreach

So you've got your website looking very smart and ready to sell tickets. Now we need to drive the traffic to your site. OK, but how?

The first thing to understand, when choosing how to communicate with your target markets, is how they want to hear from you. Do they want to get an alert via social media, see an eye-catching poster at a local store, find your announcement in the arts section of the local paper, or get a postcard with their mail? The list goes on. In your marketing plan, you will need to include a variety of media in order to reach your target markets. Nowadays, social media is an important part of the mix you will be using.

Just so we're all on the same page, what do we mean when we talk about "social media"? It does not include your email list. (We'll talk about using your email list later in this chapter.) Social media is evolving as fast as it is growing. The most wildly popular platforms today may be out of vogue by the time you are reading this. It can't be helped!

Again, what's a key thing to keep in mind as you look into platforms you'll want to use? That's right: identifying which social media are used by your target markets. In the case of community theater, it's "target markets" (plural) because you will typically be marketing both to your subscribers, who tend to be older, and to a younger target audience that you are trying to attract. You can bet that they will each have their own preferences for social media. Will you need to be on Facebook, Instagram, Twitter, YouTube, Pinterest, Reddit, Tumblr, or Snapchat? Or something newer? (Heads up: you'll want to include the topic of "media in use" when you research your customers and prospects, which we'll talk about in chapter 4.)

The best use of social media is to connect with your fans and get them talking about you. You want to connect and engage. You don't want to push ticket sales; if every tweet from your theater is just a push to buy tickets, how long will people follow you? Here are some Twitter-related ideas to get you thinking:

- We all love insider information, so tweet some quotes from your tech crew or actors while they are rehearsing or performing.
- Post photos from rehearsals or shows. On average, over one billion photos are posted to the internet every day. We are crazy for pictures!
- If you're doing a well-known show, like *Grease*, post trivia questions related to your show so everyone can show off how smart they are!

- Provide exclusive discount codes for tickets.
- Don't overlook a potential gold mine: those compelling lines in the script that just demand to be used.
- Ask followers to retweet your posts to enter a contest for free tickets. How about making it a retweet challenge?
- Remember to announce auditions for coming productions.

You'll want to create a unique hashtag for your show and encourage the cast, the production team, and everyone involved to use that hashtag. It's vital to make it a unique hashtag, so when you produce *Rent*, people will find your tweets or Instagram posts about your show and not the zillion other posts about this popular musical.

After you have identified the platforms your target markets are using, take the time to familiarize yourself with the various tools these platforms offer. The good news is that there are tools that will allow you to upload and schedule hundreds of posts at one time. You'll also encounter offers of "real-time analytics," which allow you to monitor activity as it happens on your site or app. For example, you can see the immediate effects from a blog or social network post or tweet. Depending on the platform, you will also find tools to enhance your use of photos and videos.

As soon as the run begins, you'll want to update all your digital and social media to include any reviews and, definitely, terrific quotes from your audience.

That means you need to have a way of capturing their comments in the lobby right after the curtain comes down.

Making Your CTAs Compelling

Among the things you really want to get right, using effective CTAs is high on the list. A CTA is a **call to action**. Your call to action is usually going to be "buy tickets now." Suggesting that readers retweet is another call to action. Again, you might want to do some internet searching to find examples of effective CTAs.

Here are some CTAs for non-theater products and services that might give you ideas:

Sign up for free. This wording addresses a barrier (the cost).

Join the club now. This phrase makes you feel like you've been missing out on something and implies the social benefits.

See what's next. This offers the benefit of "keeping current."

Give us a try. This wording makes the offer casual and low-risk.

Facebook

Your theater's Facebook page is probably the best place to get fans talking about your theater and shows. In a 2014 survey research report from the American Association of Community Theatre, half of the respondents said that Facebook was their preferred social media channel to receive information about the arts. While that number may change, the key message is that social media is critical in reaching your customers. As you know, that's especially true for younger customers.

Before the show opens, use pictures of rehearsals plus close-ups of set pieces and costumes to create excitement about your show. Update the Facebook page as often as possible—even daily—with interesting stories. A word to the wise: keep updates at 420 characters or less.

Those "interesting stories" can be told with videos and pictures. Shoot guerrilla-style interview videos where you pull people aside during rehearsals and ask them just a few questions. Be sure you've let your cast know that pictures and video will be shot during rehearsals. They may want to change their clothes or do their hair and makeup. With minimal editing, these could be used as teaser social media content in the weeks leading up to the show.

Your stories about the actors, director, and others working on your latest show will be livened up with their pictures. People love looking at other people, especially if they seem totally into what they are doing. The ability to tag people will help you leverage the network of everyone in the show without requiring a lot of work on their part. When your show opens, you can add pictures of packed houses. In other words, use pictures that get people to say, "I gotta see that!"

Here are some other ways to get your Facebook page working for you:

- Encourage everyone involved in your show to link to your theater's Facebook page on their personal page.
- Create some Facebook contests so more people will like and share your page.
- Join Facebook groups that will get your page seen by folks in your area who enjoy theater.

You may want to try running a Facebook ad. You'll want to test it, right? That's how you can learn how you might want to improve its effectiveness, or maybe drop it from your marketing plan. To get started, search the internet for best practices in creating Facebook ads that "convert," which means that they result in a sale.

Instagram

Is an important target of yours no longer using Facebook? That mega social network has been losing appeal with a younger **demographic**. Where have they been going? Instagram. That reflects a trend toward a more visual culture. Fortunately, theater is all about being visual!

Here's a tip about what *not* to do. Don't just slap up actors' headshots that you'll be using in your playbill, along with a list of all the shows they have ever done anywhere. That is just boring. Ask them questions such as, "What celebrity would you like to see tackle your character?" "What's the last thing you do before you go onstage?" Look again at your marketing persona's picture and think about what he or she would find interesting to read.

Marketing pros need to keep up on what's popular with their target market.

Here's an example from Newton North High School in Newton, Massachusetts (theatreinknnhs on Instagram). They post novel pictures counting down the last five days before their opening night. One included a puzzling picture, accompanied by this note: "To find out what's in this picture, come see *Spontaneous Generation*! Tickets are available online at theatreink.net." Note that they include a call to action. Good job, Newton North!

Twitter

The best use of Twitter is to broadcast what's going on with the other channels. Here are some more quick tips:

- Create a series of retweet contests to win free tickets to the show. It'll read something like this: "I want 2 free tickets to *ENTER LOVE* at Lafayette Civic on Friday 8/13. Enter to win by retweeting this message." Remember that theater is enjoyed as a social event, so give two tickets at a time, not just one.

- Aim to write tweets that are clear, witty, and succinct. If that's not your strong suit, it's never too late to look for a volunteer!
- You can show that your brand is community-minded by retweeting what's going on at other area theaters as well as other arts events, such as music, dance, and poetry slams.
- Get creative and open Twitter accounts for characters in your coming show (where copyright allows) and post funny tweets "in character."

YouTube

You can easily create a channel on YouTube and add videos. It's not something that will generate a lot of search traffic, but it is a good place to send your fans. Of course, you'll be talking about your videos on all your other social media channels. What's more, over time your collection of videos will help deliver your brand message about the quality of your shows and what people can expect from your theater.

You have all the ingredients for making a great YouTube channel: performers, sets, lighting, drama, knowledge, excitement. You not only have shows but also the behind-the-scenes stories, special events, and artists who would be only too happy to be taped doing an interview. Here is another chance to be creative and have fun! Maybe you have improv pals who'd like to create a funny sketch that ties into your current show.

Interviews can be spontaneous or formal. Vary them to widen appeal.

Here's what you will want to think about uploading:

- A quick pitch for your upcoming show
- Interviews with cast members and the leads
- Interviews with the director, choreographer, and other members of the production team
- Captivating songs or dances
- Special publicity events you've created
- Audience testimonials (Tip: Search "audience testimonials" on YouTube and judge what you think works well.)

It's possible to make your videos creative so they will get shared. For example, you might make a time-compressed video of a complex set change or the final strike (search YouTube for examples of this). There's a very funny one of the puppet wrangler for *Avenue Q* madly changing costumes on the ten puppets with a soundtrack of the *William Tell* Overture.

E-Blast Marketing

As valuable as social media is, you're also going to want to use it to bring people to your email list if you are working with a community theater. Your email list is also called your database. When you are sending marketing messages to a list, you are engaging in **e-blast marketing**. It's an important part of your marketing strategy.

Email is the first step toward building a relationship with your customers. You can think of it this way: social media is everyone at the mall, while your email database is just those people shopping in your favorite store. You've got more in common with folks in your favorite store. You're more connected. When you make an announcement to these folks, there's a good chance they will hear you.

Even though people get a lot of email, people have less mail in their inboxes than they have tweets and status updates in their newsfeed. So, if you have managed to get them to sign up for your mailing list, you have fewer competing messages. Also, you can make the messages more personal. One online marketing director remarked that email is "the easiest way to keep an ongoing dialogue with people who like our shows."

Email provides some benefits over social media. First of all, you don't have to worry about which social media platforms each person might be using. Also, you're in control. Facebook, for example, often changes the hoops you have to jump through in order for people to see what you are posting online. Another benefit to using email is that it's not only a form of direct communication but also a medium that allows you to personalize your messages.

You can use email service providers to handle subscribing/unsubscribing and the other details. With a bit of research, you can find one that best fits your goals and your budget. Or you can start out with a free service for low volume, such as MailChimp currently offers.

If you're managing your email list yourself, be sure you've done your homework and learned about the Federal Trade Commission's (FTC's) CAN-SPAM Act, which establishes requirements for commercial messages, gives recipients the right to have you stop emailing them, and spells out tough penalties for violations. An internet search should quickly take you to the right FTC page.

Growing Your List

One of your important jobs will be growing your list. Each additional person needs to have given you permission to send him or her messages. One way that someone gives you permission is by having purchased a ticket from you in the past. You need to give people the option to unsubscribe from future email contact, of course—and they will if you send boring emails! (Check with the appropriate legal professional as warranted.)

How do you grow your list? Some practical methods include:

- Place a sign-up form in your lobby. Put it in a place where people will notice it, like near the house doors, concession stand, or box office.

- Make your sign-up process more engaging. For example, offer a contest with prizes that people want: free tickets, backstage tours, a dinner with the director or members of the cast. Be sure to push your contests on social media as well.

Your database will include several groups: your subscribers (both full- and half-season), those who have bought a ticket to an individual show but not a season subscription, and those who have not yet attended a show but have somehow expressed an interest in your theater company. Another subset will be folks who volunteer or are otherwise advocates involved in your theater, and those involved in the coming show. (Remember the marketing funnel we talked about in chapter 1.)

Your advocates are often folks who would gladly help promote the show but won't really have any idea how to do that. Just for them, send weekly e-blasts with suggestions for how they can help promote the show. For example, "Thursday we are starting the retweet contest. We need your help getting the word out. Tell your family. Tell the people in your office. Get on Facebook, and tell your old high school chums." Be sure to explain the contest.

Next up is the payoff: turning your list into ticket buyers. It's helpful to look at the emails you get to learn what *you* like to receive. Make your emails something people are looking forward to. For some, this will be your calendar and a discount code. Too often, theaters think these are the only things that are of interest.

Ask yourself: What's something that they can get from us that they can't get anywhere else? If all you're doing is sending them the same thing you are sending out on social media, then there's no reason for them to read your email/newsletter. For example, you might use a camera drone to shoot footage of a bit of your production of *Wicked* and put a copy of that in your email. You can then post on Facebook, "Hey guys, we've just made an awesome drone video. Subscribe to our email list to check it out."

You'll want to start sending out announcements of a production three to four weeks before opening night. Just how do you create great e-blasts? Here's a handy "how to" list of what to have:

Clear marketing message. A good e-blast will have a clear and focused message. This one message should be in the subject line and in the email itself.

Catchy and brief subject line. Keep it to thirty characters or fewer. Examples: "*Avenue Q* Opens Soon" and "Last chance for a discount on *Wicked*." For more inspiration, just search the internet for "tips for writing great email subject lines."

Keep it brief.

Call to action. There has to be a purpose to your e-blast.

Personalization. Many email programs allow you to customize your emails so that you use the name of the person to whom you are sending the email.

NANCY COYNE

Nancy Coyne is the cofounder and chairman of Serino Coyne, the largest theatrical advertising and marketing agency in America. It has handled the marketing campaigns for such hits as *Wicked*, *The Lion King*, and *Hairspray*.

In 2007, Coyne was cited by Crain's as one of "the most powerful women in New York" for creating "virtually every Broadway advertisement for the past thirty years." At that time, her agency had 80 percent of the Broadway ad market.

She's passionate about getting people into theater seats and driving shows to become well-known brands. "We are the original reality art form," she says. "There is a live person performing for you at 8 o'clock tonight. By 11 o'clock, it's going to be over. You can't rewind. You can't listen to it over and over again. Therefore, you have to stay engaged."

Nancy Coyne poses with posters from shows she has marketed.

Coyne is a onetime child performer. After her first audition as an adult—and her first rejection—she thought, "I've got to find something else where I am deeply appreciated." She moved into advertising. Among her duties was writing spots for a small jazz radio station. She later got hired to work for Blaine Thompson. That firm handled a majority of the advertising for Broadway shows. She took what she learned and branched out on her own.

Coyne serves on the board of The Actors' Fund of America. She taught Entertainment Marketing at the Yale Drama School for many years and has also taught at Columbia University School of the Arts. In 2004, Coyne received the Tony Honor for Excellence in the Theatre.

An effective pitch for theaters is any sort of local connection—papers love a local angle. For that, find out where the director and lead actors live, as well as anyone else vital to the production. Write a press release such as "Local Actors in Musical" and include a publicity photo of the actors. If you have their permission, include contact information, so a reporter can contact the individuals for more details. A follow-up press release will need another hook, such as "Dogs Audition for *Annie*."

To get your press release used, it may be necessary for you to reach out three times: at six weeks, four weeks, and two weeks before opening night, if that's the night you want members of the press to attend.

Your posters need to be eye-catching regardless of size.

start at $20"). Consider adding a QR code (short for "quick response"). Viewers can scan it with their smartphone and learn about your production—and even buy tickets.

Your posters will probably have several lives, both as hard copy and digital. Digital versions will be used in your email and online marketing, including your website. And, of course, a simplified version will be the cover of your playbill.

Some schools like to use lawn signs to promote their shows, especially musicals, which tend to be more expensive to produce. Your school may offer to sell the signs (usually to parents) in exchange for a thank you in the program. Banners are popular for in-school promotions. They're typically placed in high-traffic areas like the cafeteria or gymnasium. Hanging a weatherproof banner outside will draw the attention of students, parents, and the community.

In-School Promotions

Some principals will allow your leads to make clever PA announcements. What about visiting the lower-level schools in your district with a special program featuring a segment of your show and some information about technical aspects, like your technical effects? Be sure to bring flyers to interest students in attending the show with their family and friends. For the right show, you might want to arrange one performance as a children's night. Hold the show an hour earlier if it's on a school night, and consider offering a discount for kids twelve or under. Backstage tours and the ability to get autographs from the leads add to the appeal.

If your high school is doing a musical, think about doing a preview of one of the show's knockout numbers during halftime at a sporting event, such as a basketball game.

Your Playbill

Creating the playbill typically is another responsibility of yours. All types of theatrical shows have playbills that contain information about the show and the performers. Most playbills also include advertisements from local businesses or messages of support to the actors and others involved in the production. Businesses

A poster can be used as a basis for a program cover.

that buy ad space can be offered comps (free tickets) in appreciation. Selling ads in a playbill is more of a PR benefit to the businesses, rather than a tactic for selling more tickets.

The cover of the playbill typically uses the artwork from the poster. Cast and crew profiles include a paragraph or two about each actor, their headshot, the shows they have done before, and whatever else that is relevant and interesting.

"Good Evening and Welcome!"

The most fun part of your job might be giving the **curtain speech**, or "preshow announcement." This is your two-minute opportunity to engage your audience with the show they are about to see. It's time to be charming, personable, and welcoming.

Your larger goal is to nurture the ongoing relationship with the audience. You'll do this by recalling recent popular productions and highlighting upcoming events. Helping regular attendees remember their pleasant experiences reinforces their positive feelings about your theater. First-timers will get an idea about the range of experiences available to them.

You may want to include an invitation that they post an update about seeing the show using your custom hashtag—before silencing their devices. Encourage patrons to text during intermission or after the final curtain.

Invite patrons to take selfies with your cast members still in costume right after the final curtain. You may want to invite them to take selfies on your

Encourage patrons to take selfies during intermission and after the show so they can inform their friends.

set. (Be sure that this is not prohibited by copyright regulations. The play or musical—as well as the set and lighting design—may have copyright protection.) Of course, the whole idea is that they post it immediately and encourage their friends to come to your show.

Curtain Up!

Opening night for short-run productions is also when you can expect reviewers. Be sure you're around to welcome them and give them any materials they might need.

The next day, send a follow-up message to the previous night's customers, possibly including a few questions. Read more about this in chapter 4.

OK, so your show is up, and opening night was a sellout. Great! But what if the rest of the shows your first weekend are not drawing the crowd you hoped for? It's time to amp up your social media. One thing that you may have now that you didn't have before is some reviews. You want to use any reviews—except if a reviewer just hated your production—in a new message or tweet.

This can be the right time to give away a few tickets. Do this by using social media to announce a new contest that grabs attention, which we've talked about before. On your Facebook page, announce an exclusive offer to your FB friends—something like, "When ordering tickets for this production, mention this offer and you'll get 25 percent off the regular ticket price."

When you're reading this, you might be thinking, "This is a lot of work." In reality, good marketing *is* a lot of work. However, you'll find it very rewarding when you see the satisfaction that comes from all sides—not just the audience, but the cast and crew—when your show is a success!

After the Run

After the set has been struck, it would be great to kick back and relax. But there's some follow-up work that needs to be done, much of which will make things easier when marketing the next show:

Contact all of the people and businesses that deserve a "thank you." These will include all your volunteers, places that posted your flyers, people in the media who ran your press releases, and reviewers.

Arrange for all posters to be removed, as well as banners, lawn signs, and the like. Members of your theater community are usually happy to help with this if you make the request.

Review the run you just finished. Document both what you did and the ticket sales. Did you get the turnout you were expecting? How do you account for that? If your numbers were low, was it really because the weather was bad? Or were some things you tried not as effective as you hoped? Go ahead and draw conclusions about what worked and what didn't, so you're always improving.

A simple survey can provide answers that settle debates about who your audience is and what that audience wants.

CHAPTER FOUR

Take It to the Next Level

Marketing research can help take your marketing efforts to the next level. You can do this in two ways. For one, you can conduct your own research. For another, you can find and use data provided by organizations that are studying topics such as trends in social media or marketing. We'll start with doing your own work, known as "custom research."

Data from marketing research can often be an effective way to convince others about your ideas. To return to an example from chapter 2's section on "Social Smarts Required," let's say you anticipate that it will be a challenge to get others to agree to the plays and musicals you'd like to put on next season.

You could create a survey (in the spring) that asks people how interested they would be in seeing a list of potential shows. The results might let you say, "We've all agreed that attracting the eighteen-to-thirty-five crowd is vital for our theater to grow. The show that generated the most interest among those eighteen to thirty-five was *Avenue Q*. So in order to attract that important younger demographic, we need to include either *Avenue Q* or a show like it." It's harder for the others to argue with data than it is for them to say, "I don't agree with you."

Postshow Research

You can begin to collect information from your audience right after the final curtain. A traditional approach has been to invite the director and some of the actors (usually the leads) to participate in a question-and-answer (Q&A). The artists sit onstage while the observers sit in the audience and ask questions for fifteen or twenty minutes.

There are other fresher approaches being tried. "Talkbacks" are gatherings in which someone (possibly you) leads the audience to share their responses. This approach gets audiences to speak to each other rather than simply to the theater or its representatives. It provides them with a second type of experience with the production. This is particularly effective when the show includes topics that provide a new viewpoint on issues of interest. In your playbill and in your curtain speech, you might also encourage your audience to tweet their reactions, using a hashtag for that specific show.

How much you will want to engage with and expand your audience will reflect the mission of your theater. For example, Studio Theater in Washington, DC, "produces plays that start conversations." In keeping with that mission, it offers several ways to encourage audience engagement, all of which provide important marketing information.

In Boston, Company One uses a variety of methods to learn how its audience is responding to its

Asking people what they liked about the show can give you great quotes for social media.

shows. It has been known to put small clipboards with surveys under every seat. It also has placed a response board in the lobby along with lots of sticky notes and pens. For one lengthy show, it was obvious that some folks were leaving during intermission. Those responsible for marketing were quick to respond. Soon there were friendly company members waiting in the lobby with charming signs asking, "Want to talk?" so they could learn why people were parachuting during intermission. This last example shows that it's possible to "gather data" in a way that is engaging rather than intrusive.

There are several benefits to sending out an email questionnaire immediately after a show. We're talking about the next day. There are multiple advantages to doing this. It lets your customers know that you value their feedback. It can provide you with quotes to use in your social media posts or on your website. It can prompt people to recommend the show to their friends. It gives you data on who attended the show (their age, gender), and learning how people heard about your show is an indication of the relative effectiveness of your marketing efforts. Lastly, the feedback can guide your selection of future projects. All of these help you improve customer satisfaction, loyalty, and advocacy.

Questions, Questions

Here are examples of questions you'd want to include:

- What are your thoughts about [name of show]?
- How likely is it that you will recommend [name of show] to a friend? (By the way, it closes on [date].)
- Did [name of show] match your expectations?
- How would you compare this to other shows you have seen us or others do?
- How did you hear about this show?
- May we use your comments on our website and/or social media to help spread the word about [name of show]?
- Demographics: gender, age group.
- Optional name and address to win a pair of tickets as a prize for completing the survey.
- During the past year, which shows did you see? (list titles)
- Whose decision was it to attend this performance? (mine, my spouse/partner's, a joint decision)

- What type of ticket did you use?
- What were the three most important reasons why you attended the performance?

Most questions should be multiple choice, since "open responses" (write what you want) are harder to analyze. You don't want to make your survey too long, or people won't complete it. Instead, you might ask some questions in one survey and different questions in the next survey.

There are free tools to enable you to conduct professional-quality surveys quickly and easily. A widely used online tool is SurveyMonkey, which allows you to send a survey with a set of ten questions and collect up to one hundred responses. It offers expert, prewritten survey templates and provides scoring of the results. Typeform is an easy-to-use form builder that is optimized for gathering feedback on mobile devices.

Free Facts

In addition to conducting your own research, there is information available from various sources. In under a minute, you can learn the demographics (age, gender, race) of people in your vicinity simply by going to American FactFinder, provided by the US Census Bureau (https://factfinder.census.gov/faces/nav/jsf/pages/index.xhtml).

If you're ready to look at lifestyles and more sophisticated measures, the Claritas MyBestSegments website provides information in a free and easy-to-use format. The Pew Research Center website has a ton

CHECKING IT TWICE

It was her first year as the marketing director of an important regional theater. There was a lot to do and a lot to think about. And since she was new, she really wanted to do a great job and impress everyone.

"Everyone" included a local playwright who had written a new play. Ah, a world-premiere event. What could be more exciting to promote!

Being a careful professional and a good team player, she was sure that she showed her press release not only to the director but also to the playwright, since he lived in the area. "Fine, lovely, perfect," she was always told.

You will be grateful every time someone catches a mistake.

She also showed them the poster, the direct mail pieces for

of free research that you can use to better understand your target market.

Getting Smart About Pricing

To demonstrate the value of using published research, we'll take a look at the topic of ticket pricing. Setting the prices for your tickets may not be your responsibility, but you definitely want to be part of the conversation. That's because buying a ticket is their subscribers, and other materials she thought warranted their attention. Of course, she first had several people proofread everything she wrote. It's just way too easy to overlook typos.

But then it happened anyway. She was ready to send the very smart-looking playbill to the printers for several thousand copies. As always, she took the time to run it by the director and the playwright, just to be sure she had their blessing.

It was the playwright who spotted it, of course. (A famous playwright, no less.) His name was misspelled. Every place it appeared. Yikes! She had missed it, and all of her proofreaders had missed it. How could that happen?

"It's an easy enough mistake," the playwright kindly assured her. As she told her story years later, you could still see the embarrassment in her face. You could also hear the promise she made to herself: always check one more time.

an important part of the relationship between your patrons and your theater. Moving people through the marketing funnel to purchase, loyalty, and then advocacy is probably the heart of your job.

This is going to sound obvious: it really matters how much you charge for a ticket. Marketing research has found out a lot more about pricing. A 2014 survey by the American Association of Community Theatre reported that pricing options and flexibility remain a vital part of each patron's decision-making process.

That means a couple of things.

- People want choices.
- Not everyone wants the same thing.
- People won't buy tickets if they can't see a price they like.
- People may spend more money if you make them the right offer.

The Marin Theatre Company in Mill Valley, California, made the papers when it decided to offer on-site babysitting services for matinees. The reporter noted, "For years (and years, and years) younger theater fans, those with families, have claimed that it was the complexity and cost of childcare that prevented them from attending live stage shows. It's Marin Theatre Company that is stepping up to the plate and offering a solution." Cleverly, the marketing professionals dubbed these "Sitter Saturdays."

A Deep Dive in How to Market to Millennials

Talking about pricing brings up the topic of getting the eighteen-to-thirty-five crowd to come to watch live theater. It's a challenge. Fewer of them attend theater than ever before; in 2012, just 13 percent reported going to the theater in the last year. (For simplicity, we're using the label "millennials," although most millennials really hate that label, or any labels.)

The Wallace Foundation provided some terrific insights in its 2017 market research study called

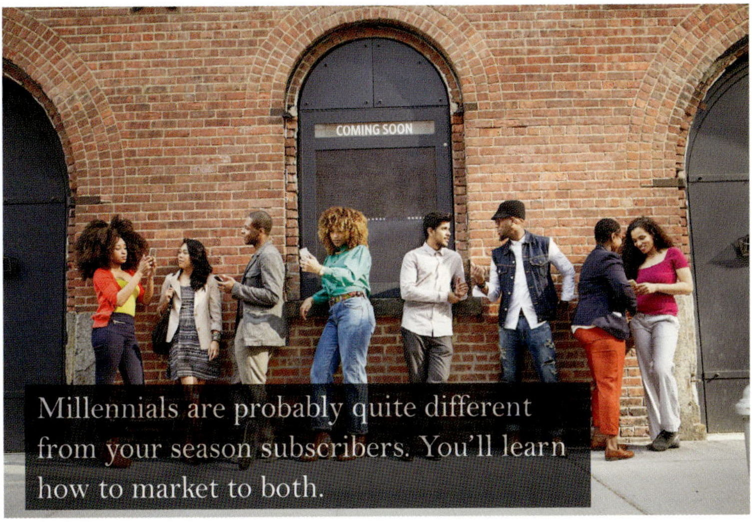

Millennials are probably quite different from your season subscribers. You'll learn how to market to both.

"Building Millennial Audiences: Barriers and Opportunities." (See For More Information for the URL.) Why is this report worth a look? You guessed it: attracting a young crowd is a challenge for those of us marketing theater. A big barrier (obstacle) is that many millennials assume that theater tickets cost more than they actually do—in fact, twice as much as the real price.

Another factor is that they are less well off than prior generations were when they were eighteen to thirty-five. Earnings are down; student loans are up. The research also found that millennials are willing to spend more freely for rock concerts or other special events they're confident they'll enjoy. They will not spend as much for an event they're not sure about, which includes theater.

How can you use that data? If you have one low rate, state it on your poster and in the media. If your theater offers a range of prices, mention the lowest one, such as "tix start at $20."

Pitching Millennials

Next up: your pitch to millennials. We talked about this in chapter 1's section "Big Idea: The Pitch." Now we'll focus on how to pitch to this specific target. You're missing an opportunity if your messaging simply says, "We're doing *Fences* this weekend, tickets going fast." To be compelling, you need to communicate the deeper benefits of seeing this play.

Research shows that millennials seek experiences that challenge them emotionally and intellectually, encourage self-discovery, and offer them a release from the stresses of everyday life. As an example, *Peerless*—a show about high school seniors competing for acceptance at an Ivy League school—has been pitched as "a spookily atmospheric psychological drama" (emotional experience) and "a chilling parable about the soul-warping price of extreme ambition" (intellectual challenge).

Let's take another example with the marketing of *Fences*. In your messages, you could talk about experiencing a son finding an ability to confront his controlling father, or a wife learning to see her husband, Troy, with new eyes. Using lines from the script may be effective in communicating something of the experience that is waiting for them, such as, "I ain't got no tears … I done spent them," which Troy reveals to his wife, Rose.

Not having someone to go with is a key reason why millennials don't go to the theater more often. Being able to have a good time with friends is an important reason for seeing their favorite performers. Now connect this with the fact that going out to a restaurant is their most popular leisure activity. What does that suggest? How about connecting your theater offering with local eateries? For example, you could offer a special "dinner & tix for two" at a discounted rate.

Buzzworthy

In your thinking about marketing to this target, focus on "buzzworthiness." Younger audiences are attracted to experiences others will like and share on social media. Buzzworthy events are those that communicate something about themselves to their followers. Millennials want to be able to talk about what they've experienced on social media and in live conversations.

As one young theatergoer tweeted: "I have tweeted about attending [organization's performance] … because I had a good time and wanted others to know how impressed I was. Also, I wanted to seem cool and cultured to my [Twitter] followers." Another who used Instagram candidly explained, "You post your

Keep a photo like this with you as a reminder of how you want others to respond to your posts.

selfie on Instagram and then make all your friends jealous. [You] feel sophisticated! There is a sense of, 'I'm awesome, I know.'"

One interesting finding in the Wallace research is that millennials say that being surrounded with others like themselves makes going someplace fun; being surrounded by older patrons does not. This suggests planning theater-going nights that are just for them.

Get Smart, Stay Smart

Marketing thinking and techniques are always evolving. You'll be smart to check out things like TED Talks to not only be inspired about the themes and subjects of future shows, but also, more broadly, to stay abreast of what some very smart people are talking about. This also means an ability to admit to and learn from your mistakes, because you will be making them. Everyone does. It's not personal.

Every job requires that you keep learning if you want to do the best job possible. That's especially important for anyone involved in marketing theater. Why? The theater community has been slower at adopting the art and science of marketing and advertising. One undeniable reason is that ads can be expensive. A thirty-second Super Bowl ad cost more than $5 million in 2017. And that's just for running it, never mind the cost of producing it.

However, with the spread of digital communication—the use of a website and social media—marketing has become more affordable for smaller organizations, such as theater companies, colleges, and schools. So theaters are now ramping up their understanding of what marketing can do for them and how to keep doing it better than ever.

The process of updating theater marketing practices presents challenges, some of which have been discussed above in "Social Smarts Required." Fortunately, there are ample ways you can improve your game. The For More Information section provides a number of resources to get you started. You might want to start with "First and Loudest: The Marketing of Broadway" on YouTube.

Other steps you'll want to take:

- When you search the internet for information on theater marketing, it helps to be specific, such as "how to sell more tickets to theatrical productions." Otherwise, you'll get a lot about marketing movies.
- Check out YouTube and other video-sharing websites to see what your competition is doing. Also, search for how various performing arts are being marketed in your area. There are some great blogs being written about marketing and marketing theater. Search with such phrases as "blogs on marketing theater," "blogs on selling theater tickets," "blogs on increasing theater subscribers." All of those will connect you with not only specific blogs to help you, but also with some bloggers you may want to follow regularly.
- Be an observer of marketing. There's marketing going on all around us, and if you pay attention, you'll be rewarded with a lot of new ideas.

Event planners are excellent at multitasking and communication, skills learned by marketing managers.

CHAPTER FIVE

The Next Act

There are many professions that you can pursue as a result of your experience working in the field of marketing and publicity for theater. The professions perhaps most commonly associated with the industry are those within consumer product companies, their agencies, and in the media, including advertising, promotions, and marketing managers; advertising sales representatives; event planners; and creative professionals. Consumer product companies are those that market products to consumers, such as tennis shoes and shampoo.

Internships

You may want to get more experience by seeking out an internship in the marketing/PR department of a regional theater. Such hands-on positions are an excellent way to expand what you know about the design and implementation of marketing campaigns. They'll offer you an opportunity to develop valuable skills in communication, relationship building, time management, and event coordination. You may be offered opportunities in:

- Community outreach: Marketing, community engagement
- Project management: Performance logistics, press events, initiatives with local artists
- Social media management: Creating conversations with the community and effectively responding to concerns and complaints

Before getting into what those professions are, let's think first about the skills you have been using and developing in theater marketing.

You're Good to Go

You've been developing a broad range of skills while marketing theater. First, there are your communication skills. You've mastered the ability to give a professional yet relaxed curtain speech to welcome each audience. Likewise, you've developed excellent interpersonal skills, also called people skills. Your work both as a team player and in dealing successfully with the public has also required active listening skills. Great listening skills are increasingly in demand.

While you may have started with a strong writing background, you've learned to vary your style with your audience. From your social media posts, you've learned to be concise and catchy. From your press releases, you have learned the value of thinking about your pitch. Your blogs have helped you focus on what your readers will find of value. Preparing materials for the media and the playbill has taught you the value of proofreading your work.

Your experience with using social media has made you familiar with a number of tools and platforms that are in widespread use in other business settings, such as:

- General office software: Microsoft Word, Excel, and PowerPoint
- Specialized software: Adobe Photoshop and desktop publishing for graphic design
- Social media platforms: Facebook, Twitter, Snapchat, Instagram, YouTube
- Email marketing platforms: Constant Contact, MailChimp
- Community management tools: Hootsuite, Sprout Social

When networking or interviewing for a career outside of theater, you'll be in a position to talk about the abilities you developed in your work in theater marketing. And those abilities are exactly the kinds that today's businesspeople are looking for. Thanks to your marketing experience, you've become adept in many, if not most, of the following areas:

- Knowing your customers and your market
- Working independently, taking the initiative
- Prioritizing projects, meeting deadlines
- Thinking creatively; being resourceful and innovative
- Exercising excellent judgment, particularly under pressure
- Using data to make decisions

- Always learning: you experiment, evaluate, and keep moving forward
- Having a strong work ethic; energetic
- Willing to be on call 24/7; flexible

Now that you've thought more about the skills and abilities used in marketing theater, let's take a quick survey of some of the professions that align with those talents.

Content Marketer

What's this all about? This new field uses nontraditional advertising/publicity methods to generate both customers and potential customers. For example, you might be working for a food company and decide to offer branded recipe books for free.

Content marketing will be a good fit for you if you've really enjoyed creating original and engaging content about your shows and working to get your online content optimized for search engines.

The demand for content marketers is huge, which is the good news. There's an even bigger boom in applicants, which is the not-so-good news. But, with your experience marketing theater to put you ahead of the others, we're back to good news!

Social Media Analyst

A social media analyst uses his or her marketing background to boost an organization's online presence through the use of social media networks and online search engine optimization (SEO). It's a growing

Social media analysts have to present findings in engaging ways.

field within marketing. Along with increased demand, there are rising expectations for skill development.

As a social media analyst, you would be studying trends in social media and using the results to inform business decisions. For example, you'd be keeping up to date on what social media platforms are popular with your target markets. You'll be expected to know what new platforms and tools are becoming available.

What you can hear in the description of a social media analyst is a commitment to learning. This will require you to know SEO practices and to understand what data you want to track. Equally important is the ability to communicate the importance of what you have learned. Meaningful reports will include the objectives you set out to meet, key findings, their implications, and your recommendations.

Marketing Researcher

Careers in marketing research tend to start within the **in-house** marketing departments of larger companies. More experienced researchers may move on to work with marketing research agencies, ad agencies, and brand consultants.

Marketing research may be a profession for you if you're curious. You've been curious about who comes to your shows and why. You wonder if a pitch was effective. You like checking to see the results of a campaign in the number of tickets sold. You've enjoyed writing surveys and learning the results. Numbers don't scare you; numbers tell you stories. These stories help you guide organizations to make smarter decisions that are focused on meeting the needs of customers.

Copywriter/Blogger

The copywriter is engaged in creating and developing advertising ideas, especially in the form of written text. You may be working in a marketing department (which is called working in-house) or for an out-of-house agency that specializes in such areas as advertising, marketing, PR, or digital media.

How do you know if copywriting is a field for you? During your time in marketing theater, you will have noticed that:

- You understand how to tell a story to different target markets.
- You have a knack for writing things in a conversational style.

Copywriters have the ability to write in different styles.

- You have the resilience to rewrite things over and over again.

Both copywriters and bloggers have the ability to write on deadline. If you need to mull, to ponder, or to debate with yourself, these "writing on demand" professions are not for you.

Graphic Designer

You may have found that you have a terrific eye for "what works." Your posters have been eye-catching. You've refreshed your theater's website to make it cleaner, clearer, and more visually compelling. You've been able to create a look for your theater across different media. All of these point to talent as a graphic designer.

Graphic designers create visual concepts to communicate ideas that inspire, inform, and engage

CHRIS BONEAU

Chris Boneau is a founding partner of Boneau/Bryan-Brown (BBB), which describes itself as "the most experienced theatrical press agency on Broadway." BBB represents such well-known productions as *Chicago*, *Stomp*, and *Mean Girls*. Boneau started out as an intern in marketing and is an example of what's possible.

His agency, BBB, currently represents *Cirque du Soleil—Paramour*. Boneau also served as Walt Disney Theatrical Productions' publicist and public relations strategist, launching Disney on Broadway. Disney's successful arrival on Broadway had a huge impact on revitalizing the theater scene in New York.

The joy Chris Boneau gets from his profession is evident.

Interestingly, Boneau heads up BBB's Media Training and Executive Presentation Coaching team. His training focuses on helping speakers to really connect with their audience and to say something meaningful.

He's drawing on years of doing both on behalf of great theater. He is also an adjunct professor at the Columbia University School of the Arts theater program.

Boneau was originally interested in acting, earning a bachelor of science in speech theater and a master of arts in acting from Louisiana State University. While working on his master's degree, he worked as an intern in the public relations and marketing department at Actors Theatre of Louisville in Kentucky.

This may explain why BBB offers internship opportunities to undergraduates and graduates "with an interest in theatre, communications, or public relations." Candidates "must be self-motivated, responsible, and well-spoken … able to work under tight deadlines in a fast-paced environment." Just like we've been talking about!

Together with his partner Adrian Bryan-Brown, Chris Boneau has represented more than four hundred plays and musicals, which have won 207 Tony Awards and nine Pulitzer Prizes. For that, Boneau deserves to take a bow!

consumers. They develop the overall layout for magazines, print ads, corporate reports, and the like. For such projects, they need to have a good understanding of typography so they can choose the appropriate font for their message.

The term graphic designer is a broad one that includes web designers, package designers, editorial designers, layout artists, and multimedia developers, among others. What they have in common is the talent and training to create visuals that communicate with their intended audience.

Public Relations

Public relations (PR) positions are most often located in companies that specialize in PR. These agencies are hired to maintain, develop, and manage the public image of their clients. They create publicity and act as a go-between with the media.

PR can be a profession to pursue if you have enjoyed either working with the press or creating events and campaigns that attract the public. Both talents are needed at a PR agency. Your PR activities for theater have included:

- Maintaining a database for the media outlets with, for example, the name and contact information for the entertainment reporter for each outlet
- Creating invitations for the press, managing the RSVPs, and sending out reminders
- For press night, creating a seating plan and getting tickets from the box office

Later in your career, you may be a PR professional, representing your clients to the media.

- Before the show, setting up the "Press Desk" where press will come to collect their tickets and pick up any materials you have prepared for them
- Monitoring coverage by the media—including print, broadcast, and online
- Seeing to it that all reviews are used (if positive) on your social media
- Thanking the reviewers

Event Planner

If you've enjoyed creating special events to promote your shows, then a career in event planning may be for you. At one end of the spectrum are small businesses that coordinate social events, such as weddings, as well as educational conferences and business meetings.

For these occasions, event planners will:

- Meet with clients to understand the purpose or goals and budget
- Propose the scope of the event, including location, program, and cost
- Coordinate every detail, from beginning to end

At the cutting edge are organizations that specialize in "experience marketing." Such agencies design engaging, interactive experiences utilizing technology such as virtual reality (VR), robotics, content analytics, animation, and more. So whether you enjoy throwing memorable parties or creating one-of-a-kind convention experiences to promote a brand, event planning may be for you.

GLOSSARY

brand Your brand is how someone thinks about your theater, based on their experiences and your reputation. Branding is what you do to influence their perception.

call to action (CTA) A request urging the viewer to take an immediate action, such as "click here to buy tickets."

curtain speech The two-minute talk before the show starts during which you want to tell your audience what they need to be safe, have fun, and connect with your theater.

database A digital file that contains the names, contact information, and other data for customers and prospects. In theater marketing, the file will include subscribers and ticket buyers, as well as other people who are considered prospects or who have a relationship with the theater.

demographics The statistical characteristics used by marketers to define their target markets. Frequently used demographics are age, gender, location, income, and marital status.

development Typically, this refers to raising money for the theater. Less often, it is used to refer to audience development, which means recruiting people to attend a performance or subscribe to the season.

dramaturge This person supports the creative team in a variety of ways, contributing an understanding of the play, its historical context, and how to communicate their vision to the audience. For a clever and informative video, go to http://dictionary.tdf.org/dramaturg.

e-blast marketing Also called email marketing, this refers to sending marketing messages to a list (most often, your database). Using an opt-in list avoids spamming, since people on these lists have chosen the option of receiving marketing messages and promotions from you through email.

in-house Work that is performed by someone who works for the organization; other tasks are done by outside agencies or vendors, such as public relations firms.

marketing An approach to doing business that focuses on what the customers feel they need or want. Theater marketers should participate in making any decisions that affect the customer, including the selection of shows, ticket pricing, the appearance of the theater, and all communications about the theater and its productions.

marketing calendar A document that lets you organize and prioritize all of your marketing activities; it should be easy to share and to update.

marketing funnel A marketing model that illustrates "the customer journey" before and after they make a purchase, which in this case is a ticket for your show.

marketing persona A fictional character who represents your customers—their demographics, their interests, their use of media, and more.

media icons Graphic symbols that represent social media sites such as Facebook and Twitter.

mission statement A written statement of an organization's purpose and focus. It communicates what is important so that everyone involved knows what he or she is trying to achieve.

pitch An attention-getting, persuasive message.

platforms The social media tools, such as Blab, Snapchat, and Twitter, that allow you to share information about your events. In marketing, it is important to use the platforms that your target market is using.

playbill The program for a performance is called a playbill. It always contains information about the production and the people involved. It may also contain advertisements.

press release Also called a "media release" or "news release," this is a short, compelling news story for newspapers and other media. For theater, this is commonly about a coming show. The internet has many examples of the standard format to use.

promotional This refers to any materials or events designed to create awareness, consideration, and purchase.

publicity Bringing news or newsworthy information about an organization to the public's attention. It's free.

public relations (PR) Any activity designed to create a favorable image of a business, its services, or its policies.

social media The websites and applications that allow people to create and share content or to participate in social networking. Traditional media include television, radio, newspapers, and periodicals.

target market A group of people identified as those most likely to become customers.

USP This stands for "unique selling proposition," which refers to a specific and unique benefit that differentiates a product or service in a way that is compelling to consumers.

FOR MORE INFORMATION

Books

Conte, David M., and Stephen Langley. *Theatre Management: Producing and Managing the Performing Arts.* Hollywood, CA: Quite Specific Media Group, 2007.

Mackowski, Christopher. *The PR Bible for Community Theatres.* Portsmouth, NH: Heinemann Drama, 2002.

Volz, Jim. *How to Run a Theater: A Witty, Practical, and Fun Guide to Arts Management.* 2nd ed. New York: Bloomsbury Methuen Drama, 2011.

Videos

Amateur Theatre: Marketing Your Company (Darlington Operatic Society: Julian Cound)
https://www.youtube.com/watch?v=gs-PiozlDKk
The marketing manager for Darlington Operatic Society talks about promoting the company's productions and overall brand.

First and Loudest: The Marketing of Broadway
https://www.youtube.com/watch?v=Eq5X60o7zlA
Experts discuss how they market, advertise, and publicize Broadway productions, including the obstacles they face and the techniques they use for creating buzz.

The Key to Social Media Success at Easton's State Theatre
https://www.youtube.com/watch?v=lHzAYmCNtI8
Jamie Balliet, senior vice president of marketing at State Theatre Center for the Arts in Easton, Pennsylvania, discusses the State Theatre's marketing strategy and how social media has been key to its success in reaching out to its patrons.

The Marketing Director (Career Guides)
https://www.youtube.com/watch?v=u8sRMz4ywG8
The American Theatre Wing and the New York Public Library for the Performing Arts produced this fifty-five-minute guide to a career as a marketing director for theater, drawing on the experience of Broadway experts.

Stephen Tartick—Marketing for Theater
https://www.youtube.com/watch?v=eo7jvna6rz4
This video features Steven Tartick, director of online marketing for Davenport Theatrical Enterprises, which produces shows for on and off Broadway.

Websites

American Association of Community Theatre
https://www.aact.org
This organization is devoted to helping theaters thrive, with expertise, assistance, networking, and support to help create the best possible experience for participants and audiences alike.

Audience Wanted
http://www.artsjournal.com/audience
Matt Lehrman, a specialist in developing audiences, writes a blog on audience development for the arts.

Educational Theatre Association
https://www.schooltheatre.org/home
A national organization of student and professional members interested in theater education; click "Community" to join more than seven thousand members sharing ideas.

Sold Out Run
http://www.soldoutrun.com
This site is packed with useful advice for marketing theater, including blogs and podcasts.

Wallace Foundation Knowledge Center
http://www.wallacefoundation.org/knowledge-center
On this site, you'll find hundreds of free reports, videos, tools, and infographics about the arts.

INDEX

Page numbers in **boldface** are illustrations. Entries in **boldface** are glossary terms.

ABOUT THE AUTHOR

George Capaccio is a theater artist with decades of experience as a writer, actor, and director. Recently, he created a one-person show as the renowned physicist Albert Einstein, which he performs in libraries, schools, universities, and other community settings. As an independent theater artist, George has employed a variety of marketing strategies to promote his programs, from creating brochures and flyers to designing his own website and publicizing his work through social media channels.